KINGFISHER
Larousse Kingfisher Chambers Inc.
95 Madison Avenue
New York, New York 10016

First American edition 1995
2 4 6 8 10 9 7 5 3 1

LIBRARY OF CONGRESS CATALOGING-IN-PUBLICATION DATA
Bell, Anthea.
[Albert le craneur. English]
Goldilocks and the three bears / written by Anthea Bell;
illustrated by Noëlle Prinz–1st American ed.
p. cm.
Summary: A retelling of the traditional tale about the little girl
who finds the house of the three bears in the woods and helps
herself to their belongings.
[1. Fairy tales. 2. folklore.] I. Prinz, Noëlle, ill.
II. Goldilocks and the three bears. English. III. Title.
PZ7.M7633Go 1995
[E] 94-48720 CIP AC

ISBN 1-85697-622-X

Stories from My Childhood

Goldilocks
· AND THE ·
Three Bears

ADAPTED FROM A STORY
BY JOSEPH CUNDALL

· ENGLISH TEXT BY ANTHEA BELL ·

· ILLUSTRATED BY NOËLLE PRINZ ·

Kingfisher
NEW YORK

Once upon a time there were Three Bears who lived together in a house in the woods: Little Bear, Middle Bear, and Big Bear. Every morning, they ate porridge for breakfast—Little Bear had a little bowl, Middle Bear had a middle-sized bowl, and Big Bear had a big bowl. They each had chairs to sit in, too: Little Bear had a little chair, Middle Bear had a middle-sized chair, and Big Bear had a big chair. At night they slept in their own beds: Little Bear had a little bed, Middle Bear had a middle-sized bed, and, of course, Big Bear had a big bed.

One morning, the Three Bears made their porridge for breakfast, poured it into their bowls and went out for a walk to give it time to cool.

While they were out, a little girl called Goldilocks came upon the bears' house. First she looked through the window, then she looked through the keyhole. Seeing no one inside she lifted the latch. The door was not locked, because the Three Bears were good bears who did no one any harm, and never thought anyone might harm them.

Goldilocks opened the door and went in. She was hungry, so she was very pleased to see the porridge on the table. If she had been a good little girl she would have waited for the bears to come home, and since they were kind bears they might have invited her to breakfast, but she was too greedy to wait.

First she tasted Big Bear's porridge. "Oh," she said, "this porridge is too hot!"

Next she tasted Middle Bear's porridge. "Oh," she said, "this porridge is too cold!"

Then she tasted Little Bear's porridge. "Good," she said. "This porridge is just right!" And she ate it all up.

Then Goldilocks sat herself down on Big Bear's chair.
"Oh," she said, "this chair is too hard!"

Next she sat down on Middle Bear's chair:
"Oh," she said, "this chair is too soft!"
Then she sat down on Little Bear's chair:
"Good," she said. "This chair is just right!"
But she must have been too heavy, for the chair fell apart.
Goldilocks landed, plop, on the floor!

After that Goldilocks went up to the Three Bears' bedroom.

First she lay down on Big Bear's bed.

"Oh," she said, "this bed is too hard!"

Next she lay down on Middle Bear's bed.

"Oh," she said, "this bed is too soft!"

Then she lay down on Little Bear's bed:

"Good," she said. "This bed is just right!"

And she settled down and fell fast asleep.

Meanwhile, the Three Bears had decided their porridge would be cool by now, so they returned home for breakfast.

But Goldilocks had left Big Bear's spoon standing in his porridge.

"Someone's been tasting my porridge!" said Big Bear in his big voice.

Then Middle Bear saw her spoon standing in her porridge too.

"Somebody's been tasting my porridge, too!" said Middle Bear in her middle-sized voice.

And Little Bear saw his spoon lying in his empty bowl.

"Somebody's been tasting my porridge and has eaten it all up!" said Little Bear in his little voice.

Now they knew that someone had been there and eaten Little Bear's breakfast, the Three Bears began looking around their house.

Goldilocks had not put the hard cushion back on Big Bear's chair quite straight.

"Somebody's been sitting on my chair!" said Big Bear in his big voice.

And Goldilocks had flattened the soft cushion in Middle Bear's chair.

"Somebody's been sitting on my chair, too!" said Middle Bear in her middle-sized voice.

And you already know what Goldilocks had done to the third chair.

"Somebody's been sitting on my chair and has broken it!" said Little Bear in his little voice.

Then the Three Bears went up to their bedroom, where Goldilocks had not put Big Bear's pillow back in the right place.

"Somebody's been lying in my bed!" said Big Bear in his big voice.

And Goldilocks had not put Middle Bear's pillow back in the right place either.

"Somebody's been lying in my bed, too!" said Middle Bear in her middle-sized voice.

When Little Bear looked at his bed, his pillow was in the right place, but in the bed lay little Goldilocks, who had no business there and was not in the right place at all.

"Somebody's been lying in my bed—and here she is!" said Little Bear in his little voice.

Goldilocks heard Big Bear's voice in her sleep, but it seemed like the roar of the wind or the rumble of thunder. And she heard Middle Bear's voice in her sleep, but it was only like hearing someone in a dream. But Little Bear's voice was so shrill that it woke her at once. She sat bolt upright, and when she saw the Three Bears standing by the bed, she tumbled out of it and ran to the window.

Luckily the window wasn't closed, because the bears always opened it in the morning to air the room. So Goldilocks jumped out and ran away into the woods, and the Three Bears never saw her again.